This Book Belongs to

Lauren

© 1985 Ron Kimball

A LITTLE HOUSE CHRISTMAS

Holiday Stories from the Little House Books

BY

LAURA INGALLS WILDER

ILLUSTRATED BY

GARTH WILLIAMS

◼ HarperCollins*Publishers*

Musical arrangement for "Merry, Merry Christmas!"
copyright © 1968 by Herbert Haufrecht

Garth Williams' artwork was colorized, with his permission, by Holly Jones.

"Little House"® is a registered trademark of HarperCollins Publishers, Inc.
U. S. Registration No. 1,771,442.

A Little House Christmas
Holiday Stories from the Little House Books

A Little House Christmas is adapted from the following books:
Little House in the Big Woods, text copyright 1932 by Laura Ingalls Wilder,
renewed 1959, 1987 by Roger L. MacBride;
pictures copyright 1953 by Garth Williams, renewed 1981by Garth Williams.
Little House on the Prairie, text copyright 1935 by Laura Ingalls Wilder,
renewed 1963, 1991 by Roger L. MacBride;
pictures copyright 1953 by Garth Williams, renewed 1981 by Garth Williams.
On the Banks of Plum Creek, text copyright 1937 by Laura Ingalls Wilder,
renewed 1965, 1993 by Roger L. MacBride;
pictures copyright 1953 by Garth Williams, renewed 1981 by Garth Williams.

Library of Congress Cataloging-in-Publication Data
Wilder, Laura Ingalls, 1867–1957.
    A Little house Christmas : holiday stories from the Little house books / by Laura Ingalls Wilder ; illustrated by Garth Williams.
        p.   cm.
    Summary: A collection of stories that describe the experiences of a pioneer girl and her family as they celebrate various Christmases in the Big Woods in Wisconsin, on the prairie in Indian Territory, and on the banks of Plum Creek.
    ISBN 0-06-024269-8. — ISBN 0-06-024270-1 (lib. bdg.)
    [1. Children's stories, American.   2. Christmas—Fiction.   3. Frontier and pioneer life—Fiction. 4. Family life—Fiction.]   I. Williams, Garth, ill. II. Title.
PZ7.W6461Lg   1994   93-24537
[Fic]—dc20   CIP
                                                                                                                          AC

Typography by Christine Hoffman
1   2   3   4   5   6   7   8   9   10
❖
First Edition

CONTENTS

ONCE UPON A TIME, *a little girl named Laura Ingalls lived in a little log cabin in the Big Woods of Wisconsin with her Pa, her Ma, her big sister Mary, and her baby sister Carrie. Laura had many adventures as she traveled west across the prairie with her family in their covered wagon, and when Laura was grown, she told of these adventures in the Little House books. Some of the most wonderful stories in these books are those that tell of the merry Christmas celebrations in the little houses in the Big Woods of Wisconsin, on the Kansas prairie, and on the banks of beautiful Plum Creek in Minnesota. Here are all of the special Christmas stories from those long-ago days, gathered together in one holiday storybook. Merry Christmas, Laura!*

Christmas in the Big Woods

It's wintertime in the Big Woods of Wisconsin, and a little log cabin deep in the woods is practically covered with snow. Inside the cabin a little girl named Laura Ingalls is very excited, because Christmas is almost here! Laura is only four years old, but she's big enough to help her Pa, her Ma, and her big sister Mary get the little house ready for Christmas visitors. It's very cold and snowy outside, but Laura and Mary know that Santa Claus will be coming soon with all sorts of Christmas treasures.

Christmas

Christmas was coming.

The little log house was almost buried in snow. Great drifts were banked against the walls and windows, and in the morning when Pa opened the door, there was a wall of snow as high as Laura's head. Pa took the shovel and shoveled it away, and then he shoveled a path to the barn, where the horses and the cows were snug and warm in their stalls.

The days were clear and bright. Laura and Mary stood on chairs by the window and looked out across the glittering snow at the glittering trees. Snow was piled all along their bare, dark branches, and it sparkled in the sunshine. Icicles hung from the eaves of the house to the snowbanks, great icicles as large at the top as Laura's arm. They were like glass and full of sharp lights.

Pa's breath hung in the air like smoke, when he came along the path from the barn. He breathed it out in clouds and it froze in white frost on his mustache and beard.

When he came in, stamping the snow from his boots, and caught Laura up in a bear's hug against his cold, big coat, his mustache was beaded with little drops of melting frost.

Every night he was busy, working on a large piece of board and two small pieces. He whittled them with his knife, he rubbed them with sandpaper and with the palm of his hand, until when Laura touched them they felt soft and smooth as silk.

Then with his sharp jack-knife he worked at them, cutting the edges of the large one into little peaks and towers, with a large star carved on the very tallest point. He cut little holes through the wood. He cut the holes in shapes of windows, and little stars, and crescent moons, and circles. All around them he carved tiny leaves, and flowers, and birds.

One of the little boards he shaped in a lovely curve, and around its edges he carved leaves and flowers and stars, and through it he cut crescent moons and curlicues.

Around the edges of the smallest board he carved a tiny flowering vine.

He made the tiniest shavings, cutting very slowly and carefully, making whatever he thought would be pretty.

At last he had the pieces finished and one night he fitted them together. When this was done, the large piece was a beautifully carved back for a smooth little shelf across its middle. The large star was at the very top of it. The curved piece supported the shelf underneath, and it was carved beautifully, too. And the little vine ran around the edge of the shelf.

Pa had made this bracket for a Christmas present for Ma. He hung it carefully against the log wall between the windows, and Ma stood her little china woman on the shelf.

The little china woman had a china bonnet on her head, and china curls hung against her china neck. Her china dress was laced across in front, and she wore a pale pink china apron and little gilt china shoes. She was beautiful, standing on the shelf with flowers and leaves and birds and moons carved all around her, and the large star at the very top.

Ma was busy all day long, cooking good things for Christmas. She

baked salt-rising bread and rye'n'Injun bread, and Swedish crackers, and a huge pan of baked beans, with salt pork and molasses. She baked vinegar pies and dried-apple pies, and filled a big jar with cookies, and she let Laura and Mary lick the cake spoon.

One morning she boiled molasses and sugar together until they made a thick syrup, and Pa brought in two pans of clean, white snow from outdoors. Laura and Mary each had a pan, and Pa and Ma showed them how to pour the dark syrup in little streams onto the snow.

They made circles, and curlicues, and squiggledy things, and these hardened at once and were candy. Laura and Mary might eat one piece each, but the rest was saved for Christmas Day.

All this was done because Aunt Eliza and Uncle Peter and the cousins, Peter and Alice and Ella, were coming to spend Christmas.

The day before Christmas they came. Laura and Mary heard the gay ringing of sleigh bells, growing louder every moment, and then the big bobsled came out of the woods and drove up to the gate. Aunt Eliza and Uncle Peter and the cousins were in it, all covered up, under blankets and robes and buffalo skins.

They were wrapped up in so many coats and mufflers and veils and shawls that they looked like big, shapeless bundles.

When they all came in, the little house was full and running over. Black Susan ran out and hid in the barn, but Jack leaped in circles through the snow, barking as though he would never stop. Now there were cousins to play with!

As soon as Aunt Eliza had unwrapped them, Peter and Alice and Ella and Laura and Mary began to run and shout. At last Aunt Eliza told them to be quiet. Then Alice said:

"I'll tell you what let's do. Let's make pictures."

Alice said they must go outdoors to do it, and Ma thought it was too cold for Laura to play outdoors. But when she saw how disappointed Laura was, she said she might go, after all, for a little while. She put on Laura's coat and mittens and the warm cape with the hood, and wrapped a muffler around her neck, and let her go.

Laura had never had so much fun. All morning she played outdoors in the snow with Alice and Ella and Peter and Mary, making pictures. The way they did it was this:

Each one by herself climbed up on a stump, and then all at once, holding their arms out wide, they fell off the stumps into the soft, deep snow. They fell flat on their faces. Then they tried to get up without spoiling the marks they made when they fell. If they did it well, there in the snow were five holes, shaped almost exactly like four little girls and a boy, arms and legs and all. They called these their pictures.

They played so hard all day that when night came they were too excited to sleep. But they must sleep, or Santa Claus would not come. So they hung their stockings by the fireplace, and said their prayers, and went to bed—Alice and Ella and Mary and Laura all in one big bed on the floor.

Peter had the trundle bed. Aunt Eliza and Uncle Peter were going to sleep in the big bed, and another bed was made on the attic floor for Pa

and Ma. The buffalo robes and all the blankets had been brought in from Uncle Peter's sled, so there were enough covers for everybody.

Pa and Ma and Aunt Eliza and Uncle Peter sat by the fire, talking. And just as Laura was drifting off to sleep, she heard Uncle Peter say:

"Eliza had a narrow squeak the other day, when I was away at Lake

City. You know Prince, that big dog of mine?"

Laura was wide awake at once. She always liked to hear about dogs. She lay still as a mouse, and looked at the fire-light flickering on the log walls, and listened to Uncle Peter.

"Well," Uncle Peter said, "early in the morning Eliza started to the spring to get a pail of water, and Prince was following her. She got to the edge of the ravine, where the path goes down to the spring, and all of a sudden Prince set his teeth in the back of her skirt and pulled.

"You know what a big dog he is. Eliza scolded him, but he wouldn't let go, and he's so big and strong she couldn't get away from him. He kept backing and pulling, till he tore a piece out of her skirt."

"It was my blue print," Aunt Eliza said to Ma.

"Dear me!" Ma said.

"He tore a big piece right out of the back of it," Aunt Eliza said. "I was so mad I could have whipped him for it. But he growled at me."

"Prince growled at you?" Pa said.

"Yes," said Aunt Eliza.

"So then she started on again toward the spring," Uncle Peter went on. "But Prince jumped into the path ahead of her and snarled at her. He paid no attention to her talking and scolding. He just kept on showing his teeth and snarling, and when she tried to get past him he kept in front of her and snapped at her. That scared her."

"I should think it would!" Ma said.

"He was so savage, I thought he was going to bite me," said Aunt Eliza. "I believe he would have."

"I never heard of such a thing!" said Ma. "What on earth did you do?"

"I turned right around and ran into the house where the children were, and slammed the door," Aunt Eliza answered.

"Of course Prince was savage with strangers," said Uncle Peter. "But he was always so kind to Eliza and the children I felt perfectly safe to leave them with him. Eliza couldn't understand it at all.

"After she got into the house he kept pacing around it and growling. Every time she started to open the door he jumped at her and snarled."

"Had he gone mad?" said Ma.

"That's what I thought," Aunt Eliza said. "I didn't know what to do. There I was, shut up in the house with the children, and not daring to go out. And we didn't have any water. I couldn't even get any snow to melt. Every time I opened the door so much as a crack, Prince acted like he would tear me to pieces."

"How long did this go on?" Pa asked.

"All day, till late in the afternoon," Aunt Eliza said. "Peter had taken the gun, or I would have shot him."

"Along late in the afternoon," Uncle Peter said, "he got quiet, and lay down in front of the door. Eliza thought he was asleep, and she made up her mind to try to slip past him and get to the spring for some water.

"So she opened the door very quietly, but of course he woke up right away. When he saw she had the water pail in her hand, he got up and walked ahead of her to the spring, just the same as usual. And there, all around the spring in the snow, were the fresh tracks of a panther."

"The tracks were as big as my hand," said Aunt Eliza.

"Yes," Uncle Peter said, "he was a big fellow. His tracks were the biggest I ever saw. He would have got Eliza sure, if Prince had let her go to the spring in the morning. I saw the tracks. He had been lying up in that big oak over the spring, waiting for some animal to come there for water. Undoubtedly he would have dropped down on her.

"Night was coming on, when she saw the tracks, and she didn't waste any time getting back to the house with her pail of water. Prince followed close behind her, looking back into the ravine now and then."

"I took him into the house with me," Aunt Eliza said, "and we all stayed inside, till Peter came home."

"Did you get him?" Pa asked Uncle Peter.

"No," Uncle Peter said. "I took my gun and hunted all round the place, but I couldn't find him. I saw some more of his tracks. He'd gone on north, farther into the Big Woods."

Alice and Ella and Mary were all wide awake now, and Laura put her head under the covers and whispered to Alice, "My! weren't you scared?"

Alice whispered back that she was scared, but Ella was scareder. And Ella whispered that she wasn't, either, any such thing.

"Well, anyway, you made more fuss about being thirsty," Alice whispered.

They lay there whispering about it till Ma said: "Charles, those children never will get to sleep unless you play for them." So Pa got his fiddle.

The room was still and warm and full of fire-light. Ma's shadow, and Aunt Eliza's and Uncle Peter's were big and quivering on the walls in the flickering fire-light, and Pa's fiddle sang merrily to itself.

It sang "Money Musk," and "The Red Heifer," "The Devil's Dream," and "Arkansas Traveler." And Laura went to sleep while Pa and the fiddle were both softly singing:

> *"My darling Nelly Gray, they have taken you away,*
> *And I'll never see my darling any more. . . ."*

In the morning they all woke up almost at the same moment. They looked at their stockings, and something was in them. Santa Claus had been there. Alice and Ella and Laura in their red flannel nightgowns, and Peter in his red flannel nightshirt, all ran shouting to see what he had brought.

In each stocking there was a pair of bright red mittens, and there was a long, flat stick of red-and-white-striped peppermint candy, all beautifully notched along each side.

They were all so happy they could hardly speak at first. They just looked with shining eyes at those lovely Christmas presents. But Laura was happiest of all. Laura had a rag doll.

She was a beautiful doll. She had a face of white cloth with black button eyes. A black pencil had made her eyebrows, and her cheeks and her mouth were red with the ink made from pokeberries. Her hair was black yarn that had been knit and raveled, so that it was curly.

She had little red flannel stockings and little black cloth gaiters for shoes, and her dress was pretty pink and blue calico.

She was so beautiful that Laura could not say a word. She just held her tight and forgot everything else. She did not know that everyone was looking at her, till Aunt Eliza said:

"Did you ever see such big eyes!"

The other girls were not jealous because Laura had mittens, and candy, *and* a doll, because Laura was the littlest girl, except Baby Carrie and Aunt Eliza's little baby, Dolly Varden. The babies were too small for dolls. They were so small they did not even know about Santa Claus.

They just put their fingers in their mouths and wriggled because of all the excitement.

Laura sat down on the edge of the bed and held her doll. She loved her red mittens and she loved the candy, but she loved her doll best of all. She named her Charlotte.

Then they all looked at each other's mittens, and tried on their own, and Peter bit a large piece out of his stick of candy, but Alice and Ella and Mary and Laura licked theirs, to make it last longer.

"Well, well!" Uncle Peter said. "Isn't there even one stocking with nothing but a switch in it? My, my, have you all been such good children?"

But they didn't believe that Santa Claus could, really, have given any of them nothing but a switch. That happened to some children, but it couldn't happen to them. It was so hard to be good all the time, every day, for a whole year.

"You mustn't tease the children, Peter," Aunt Eliza said.

Ma said, "Laura, aren't you going to let the other girls hold your doll?" She meant, "Little girls must not be so selfish."

So Laura let Mary take the beautiful doll, and then Alice held her a minute, and then Ella. They smoothed the pretty dress and admired the red flannel stockings and the gaiters, and the curly woolen hair. But Laura was glad when at last Charlotte was safe in her arms again.

Pa and Uncle Peter had each a pair of new, warm mittens, knit in little squares of red and white. Ma and Aunt Eliza had made them.

Aunt Eliza had brought Ma a large red apple stuck full of cloves. How good it smelled! And it would not spoil, for so many cloves would keep it sound and sweet.

Ma gave Aunt Eliza a little needle-book she had made, with bits of silk for covers and soft white flannel leaves into which to stick the needles. The flannel would keep the needles from rusting.

They all admired Ma's beautiful bracket, and Aunt Eliza said that Uncle Peter had made one for her—of course, with different carving.

Santa Claus had not given them anything at all. Santa Claus did not give grown people presents, but that was not because they had not been good. Pa and Ma were good. It was because they were grown up, and grown people must give each other presents.

Then all the presents must be laid away for a little while. Peter went out with Pa and Uncle Peter to do the chores, and Alice and Ella helped Aunt Eliza make the beds, and Laura and Mary set the table, while Ma got breakfast.

For breakfast there were pancakes, and Ma made a pancake man for each one of the children. Ma called each one in turn to bring her plate, and each could stand by the stove and watch, while with the spoonful of batter Ma put on the arms and the legs and the head. It was exciting to watch her turn the whole little man over, quickly and carefully, on a hot griddle. When it was done, she put it smoking hot on the plate.

Peter ate the head off his man, right away. But Alice and Ella and Mary and Laura ate theirs slowly in little bits, first the arms and legs and then the middle, saving the head for the last.

Today the weather was so cold that they could not play outdoors, but there were the new mittens to admire, and the candy to lick. And they all sat on the floor together and looked at the pictures in the Bible, and the pictures of all kinds of animals and birds in Pa's big green book. Laura kept Charlotte in her arms the whole time.

Then there was the Christmas dinner. Alice and Ella and Peter and Mary and Laura did not say a word at table, for they knew that children should be seen and not heard. But they did not need to ask for second helpings. Ma and Aunt Eliza kept their plates full and let them eat all the good things they could hold.

"Christmas comes but once a year," said Aunt Eliza.

Dinner was early, because Aunt Eliza, Uncle Peter, and the cousins had such a long way to go.

"Best the horses can do," Uncle Peter said, "we'll hardly make it home before dark."

So as soon as they had eaten dinner, Uncle Peter and Pa went to put the horses to the sled, while Ma and Aunt Eliza wrapped up the cousins.

They pulled heavy woolen stockings over the woolen stockings and the shoes they were already wearing. They put on mittens and coats and warm hoods and shawls, and wrapped mufflers around their necks and thick woolen veils over their faces. Ma slipped piping hot baked potatoes into their pockets to keep their fingers warm, and Aunt Eliza's flatirons were hot on the stove, ready to put at their feet in the sled. The blankets and the quilts and the buffalo robes were warmed, too.

So they all got into the big bobsled, cosy and warm, and Pa tucked the last robe well in around them.

"Good-by! Good-by!" they called, and off they went, the horses trotting gaily and the sleigh bells ringing.

In just a little while the merry sound of the bells was gone, and Christmas was over. But what a happy Christmas it had been!

CHRISTMAS ON THE PRAIRIE

Laura is six years old now, and she and her folks have traveled in their covered wagon all the way from the Big Woods of Wisconsin to a new little house, this one on the wide-open prairie in Indian Territory. Cold rain has been falling for days and days, and Laura and Mary are very worried, for they know Santa Claus needs snow in order to visit the little house on the prairie. But Christmas is almost here, and there is no sign of snow anywhere—only more and more rain from the cold, gray skies. Will there be no Christmas this year?

Mr. Edwards Meets Santa Claus

The days were short and cold, the wind whistled sharply, but there was no snow. Cold rains were falling. Day after day the rain fell, pattering on the roof and pouring from the eaves.

Mary and Laura stayed close by the fire, sewing their nine-patch quilt blocks, or cutting paper dolls from scraps of wrapping-paper, and hearing the wet sound of the rain. Every night was so cold that they expected to see snow next morning, but in the morning they saw only sad, wet grass.

They pressed their noses against the squares of glass in the windows that Pa had made, and they were glad they could see out. But they wished they could see snow.

Laura was anxious because Christmas was near, and Santa Claus and his reindeer could not travel without snow. Mary was afraid that, even if it snowed, Santa Claus could not find them, so far away in Indian Territory. When they asked Ma about this, she said she didn't know.

"What day is it?" they asked her, anxiously. "How many more days till Christmas?" And they counted off the days on their fingers, till there was only one more day left.

Rain was still falling that morning. There was not one crack in the gray sky. They felt almost sure there would be no Christmas. Still, they kept hoping.

Just before noon the light changed. The clouds broke and drifted apart, shining white in a clear blue sky. The sun shone, birds sang, and thousands of drops of water sparkled on the grasses. But when Ma opened the door to let in the fresh, cold air, they heard the creek roaring.

They had not thought about the creek. Now they knew they would have no Christmas, because Santa Claus could not cross that roaring creek.

Pa came in, bringing a big fat turkey. If it weighed less than twenty pounds, he said, he'd eat it, feathers and all. He asked Laura, "How's that for a Christmas dinner? Think you can manage one of those drumsticks?"

She said, yes, she could. But she was sober. Then Mary asked him if the creek was going down, and he said it was still rising.

Ma said it was too bad. She hated to think of Mr. Edwards eating his bachelor cooking all alone on Christmas day. Mr. Edwards had been asked to eat Christmas dinner with them, but Pa shook his head and said a man would risk his neck, trying to cross that creek now.

"No," he said. "That current's too strong. We'll just have to make up our minds that Edwards won't be here tomorrow."

Of course that meant that Santa Claus could not come, either.

Laura and Mary tried not to mind too much. They watched Ma dress the wild turkey, and it was a very fat turkey. They were lucky little girls, to have a good house to live in, and a warm fire to sit by, and such a turkey for their Christmas dinner. Ma said so, and it was true. Ma said it was too bad that Santa Claus couldn't come this year, but they were such good girls that he hadn't forgotten them; he would surely come next year.

Still, they were not happy.

After supper that night they washed their hands and faces, buttoned their red-flannel nightgowns, tied their night-cap strings, and soberly said their prayers. They lay down in bed and pulled the covers up. It did not seem at all like Christmas time.

Pa and Ma sat silent by the fire. After a while Ma asked why Pa didn't play the fiddle, and he said, "I don't seem to have the heart to, Caroline."

After a longer while, Ma suddenly stood up.

"I'm going to hang up your stockings, girls," she said. "Maybe something will happen."

Laura's heart jumped. But then she thought again of the creek and she knew nothing could happen.

Ma took one of Mary's clean stockings and one of Laura's, and she hung them from the mantel-shelf, on either side of the fireplace. Laura and Mary watched her over the edge of their bed-covers.

"Now go to sleep," Ma said, kissing them good night. "Morning will come quicker if you're asleep."

She sat down again by the fire and Laura almost went to sleep. She woke up a little when she heard Pa say, "You've only made it worse, Caroline." And she thought she heard Ma say: "No, Charles. There's the white sugar." But perhaps she was dreaming.

Then she heard Jack growl savagely. The door-latch rattled and someone said, "Ingalls! Ingalls!" Pa was stirring up the fire, and when he opened the door Laura saw that it was morning. The outdoors was gray.

"Great fishhooks, Edwards! Come in, man! What's happened?" Pa exclaimed.

Laura saw the stockings limply dangling, and she scrooged her shut eyes into the pillow. She heard Pa piling wood on the fire, and she heard Mr. Edwards say he had carried his clothes on his head when he swam the creek. His teeth rattled and his voice shivered. He would be all right, he said, as soon as he got warm.

"It was too big a risk, Edwards," Pa said. "We're glad you're here, but that was too big a risk for a Christmas dinner."

"Your little ones had to have a Christmas," Mr. Edwards replied. "No creek could stop me, after I fetched them their gifts from Independence."

Laura sat straight up in bed. "Did you see Santa Claus?" she shouted.

"I sure did," Mr. Edwards said.

"Where? When? What did he look like? What did he say? Did he really give you something for us?" Mary and Laura cried.

"Wait, wait a minute!" Mr. Edwards laughed. And Ma said she would put the presents in the stockings, as Santa Claus intended. She said they mustn't look.

Mr. Edwards came and sat on the floor by their bed, and he answered every question they asked him. They honestly tried not to look at Ma, and they didn't quite see what she was doing.

When he saw the creek rising, Mr. Edwards said, he had known that Santa Claus could not get across it. ("But you crossed it," Laura said. "Yes," Mr. Edwards replied, "but Santa Claus is too old and fat. He couldn't make it, where a long, lean razor-back like me could do so.") And

30

Mr. Edwards reasoned that if Santa Claus couldn't cross the creek, likely he would come no farther south than Independence. Why should he come forty miles across the prairie, only to be turned back? Of course he wouldn't do that!

So Mr. Edwards had walked to Independence. ("In the rain?" Mary asked. Mr. Edwards said he wore his rubber coat.) And there, coming down the street in Independence, he had met Santa Claus. ("In the daytime?" Laura asked. She hadn't thought that anyone could see Santa Claus in the daytime. No, Mr. Edwards said; it was night, but light shone out across the street from the saloons.)

Well, the first thing Santa Claus said was, "Hello, Edwards!" ("Did he know you?" Mary asked, and Laura asked, "How did you know he was really Santa Claus?" Mr. Edwards said that Santa Claus knew everybody. And he had recognized Santa at once by his whiskers. Santa Claus had the longest, thickest, whitest set of whiskers west of the Mississippi.)

So Santa Claus said, "Hello, Edwards! Last time I saw you you were sleeping on a corn-shuck bed in Tennessee." And Mr. Edwards well remembered the little pair of red-yarn mittens that Santa Claus had left for him that time.

Then Santa Claus said: "I understand you're living now down along the Verdigris River. Have you ever met up, down yonder, with two little young girls named Mary and Laura?"

"I surely am acquainted with them," Mr. Edwards replied.

"It rests heavy on my mind," said Santa Claus. "They are both of them sweet, pretty, good little young things, and I know they are expecting me. I surely do hate to disappoint two good little girls like them. Yet with the water up the way it is, I can't ever make it across that creek. I can figure no way whatsoever to get to their cabin this year. Edwards," Santa Claus said. "Would you do me the favor to fetch them their gifts this one time?"

"I'll do that, and with pleasure," Mr. Edwards told him.

Then Santa Claus and Mr. Edwards stepped across the street to the hitching-posts where the pack-mule was tied. ("Didn't he have his reindeer?" Laura asked. "You know he couldn't," Mary said. "There isn't any snow." Exactly, said Mr. Edwards. Santa Claus traveled with a pack-mule in the southwest.)

And Santa Claus uncinched the pack and looked through it, and he took out the presents for Mary and Laura.

"Oh, what are they?" Laura cried; but Mary asked, "Then what did he do?"

Then he shook hands with Mr. Edwards, and he swung up on his fine bay horse. Santa Claus rode well for a man of his weight and build. And he tucked his long, white whiskers under his bandana. "So long, Edwards," he said, and he rode away on the Fort Dodge trail, leading

his pack-mule and whistling.

Laura and Mary were silent an instant, thinking of that.

Then Ma said, "You may look now, girls."

Something was shining bright in the top of Laura's stocking. She squealed and jumped out of bed. So did Mary, but Laura beat her to the fireplace. And the shining thing was a glittering new tin cup.

Mary had one exactly like it.

These new tin cups were their very own. Now they each had a cup to drink out of. Laura jumped up and down and shouted and laughed, but Mary stood still and looked with shining eyes at her own tin cup.

Then they plunged their hands into the stockings again. And they pulled out two long, long sticks of candy. It was peppermint candy, striped red and white. They looked and looked at the beautiful candy, and Laura licked her stick, just one lick. But Mary was not so greedy. She didn't take even one lick of her stick.

Those stockings weren't empty yet. Mary and Laura pulled out two small packages. They unwrapped them, and each found a little heart-shaped cake. Over their delicate brown tops was sprinkled white sugar. The sparkling grains lay like tiny drifts of snow.

34

The cakes were too pretty to eat. Mary and Laura just looked at them. But at last Laura turned hers over, and she nibbled a tiny nibble from underneath, where it wouldn't show. And the inside of the little cake was white!

It had been made of pure white flour, and sweetened with white sugar.

Laura and Mary never would have looked in their stockings again. The cups and the cakes and the candy were almost too much. They were too happy to speak. But Ma asked if they were sure the stockings were empty.

Then they put their hands down inside them, to make sure.

And in the very toe of each stocking was a shining bright, new penny!

They had never even thought of such a thing as having a penny. Think

of having a whole penny for your very own. Think of having a cup and a cake and a stick of candy *and* a penny.

There never had been such a Christmas.

Now of course, right away, Laura and Mary should have thanked Mr. Edwards for bringing those lovely presents all the way from Independence. But they had forgotten all about Mr. Edwards. They had even forgotten Santa Claus. In a minute they would have remembered, but before they did, Ma said, gently, "Aren't you going to thank Mr. Edwards?"

"Oh, thank you, Mr. Edwards! Thank you!" they said, and they meant it with all their hearts. Pa shook Mr. Edwards' hand, too, and shook it again. Pa and Ma and Mr. Edwards acted as if they were almost crying, Laura didn't know why. So she gazed again at her beautiful presents.

She looked up again when Ma gasped. And Mr. Edwards was taking sweet potatoes out of his pockets. He said they had helped to balance the package on his head when he swam across the creek. He thought Pa and Ma might like them, with the Christmas turkey.

There were nine sweet potatoes. Mr. Edwards had brought them all the way from town, too. It was just too much. Pa said so. "It's too much, Edwards," he said. They never could thank him enough.

Mary and Laura were too excited to eat breakfast. They drank the milk from their shining new cups, but they could not swallow the rabbit stew and the cornmeal mush.

"Don't make them, Charles," Ma said. "It will soon be dinner-time."

For Christmas dinner there was the tender, juicy, roasted turkey. There were the sweet potatoes, baked in the ashes and carefully wiped so that you could eat the good skins, too. There was a loaf of salt-rising bread made from the last of the white flour.

And after all that there were stewed dried blackberries and little cakes. But these little cakes were made with brown sugar and they did not have white sugar sprinkled over their tops.

Then Pa and Ma and Mr. Edwards sat by the fire and talked about Christmas times back in Tennessee and up north in the Big Woods. But Mary and Laura looked at their beautiful cakes and played with their pennies and drank their water out of their new cups. And little by little they licked and sucked their sticks of candy, till each stick was sharp-pointed on one end.

That was a happy Christmas.

CHRISTMAS
ON
PLUM CREEK

The Ingalls family has packed up the covered wagon once again and moved from the little house on the prairie to a little sod house on the banks of Plum Creek in Minnesota. Eight-year-old Laura is a bit worried that there is no fireplace or chimney in the little sod house, but she and Mary are sure that Santa Claus will find them anyway. And they know just what they want for Christmas this year—until Ma helps them understand the special meaning of Christmas wishes.

The Christmas Horses

Grasshopper weather was strange weather. Even at Thanksgiving, there was no snow.

The door of the dugout was wide open while they ate Thanksgiving dinner. Laura could see across the bare willow-tops, far over the prairie to the place where the sun would go down. There was not one speck of snow. The prairie was like soft yellow fur. The line where it met the sky was not sharp now; it was smudged and blurry.

"Grasshopper weather," Laura thought to herself. She thought of grasshoppers' long, folded wings and their high-jointed hind legs. Their feet were thin and scratchy. Their heads were hard, with large eyes on the corners, and their jaws were tiny and nibbling.

If you caught a grasshopper and held him, and gently poked a green blade of grass into his jaws, they nibbled it fast. They swiftly nibbled in the whole grass blade, till the tip of it went into them and was gone.

Thanksgiving dinner was good. Pa had shot a wild goose for it. Ma had to stew the goose because there was no fireplace, and no oven in the little stove. But she made dumplings in the gravy. There were corn dodgers and mashed potatoes. There were butter, and milk, and stewed dried plums. And three grains of parched corn lay beside each tin plate.

At the first Thanksgiving dinner the poor Pilgrims had nothing to eat but three parched grains of corn. Then the Indians came and brought them turkeys, so the Pilgrims were thankful.

Now, after they had eaten their good, big Thanksgiving dinner, Laura and Mary could eat their grains of corn and remember the Pilgrims. Parched corn was good. It crackled and crunched, and its taste was sweet and brown.

Then Thanksgiving was past and it was time to think of Christmas. Still there was no snow and no rain. The sky was gray, the prairie was dull, and the winds were cold. But the cold winds blew over the top of the dugout.

"A dugout is snug and cosy," said Ma. "But I do feel like an animal penned up for the winter."

"Never mind, Caroline," Pa said. "We'll have a good house next year." His eyes shone and his voice was like singing. "And good horses, and a buggy to boot! I'll take you riding, dressed up in silks! Think, Caroline—this level, rich land, not a stone or stump to contend with, and only three miles from a railroad! We can sell every grain of wheat we raise!"

Then he ran his fingers through his hair and said, "I do wish I had a team of horses."

"Now, Charles," said Ma. "Here we are, all healthy and safe and snug, with food for the winter. Let's be thankful for what we have."

"I am," Pa said. "But Pete and Bright are too slow for harrowing and harvesting. I've broken up that big field with them, but I can't put it all in wheat, without horses."

Then Laura had a chance to speak without interrupting. She said, "There isn't any fireplace."

"Whatever are you talking about?" Ma asked her.

"Santa Claus," Laura answered.

"Eat your supper, Laura, and let's not cross bridges till we come to them," said Ma.

Laura and Mary knew that Santa Claus could not come down a chimney where there was no chimney. One day Mary asked Ma how Santa Claus would come. Ma did not answer. Instead, she asked, "What do you girls want for Christmas?"

She was ironing. One end of the ironing-board was on the table and the other on the bedstead. Pa had made the bedstead that high, on purpose. Carrie was playing on the bed and Laura and Mary sat at the table. Mary was sorting quilt blocks and Laura was making a little apron for the rag doll, Charlotte. The wind howled overhead and whined in the stovepipe, but there was no snow yet.

Laura said, "I want candy."

"So do I," said Mary, and Carrie cried, "Tandy?"

"And a new winter dress, and a coat, and a hood," said Mary.

"So do I," said Laura. "And a dress for Charlotte, and—"

Ma lifted the iron from the stove and held it out to them. They could test the iron. They licked their fingers and touched them, quicker than quick, to the smooth hot bottom. If it crackled, the iron was hot enough.

"Thank you, Mary and Laura," Ma said. She began carefully ironing around and over the patches on Pa's shirt. "Do you know what Pa wants for Christmas?"

They did not know.

"Horses," Ma said. "Would you girls like horses?"

Laura and Mary looked at each other.

"I only thought," Ma went on, "if we all wished for horses, and nothing but horses, then maybe—"

Laura felt queer. Horses were everyday; they were not Christmas. If Pa got horses, he would trade for them. Laura could not think of Santa Claus and horses at the same time.

"Ma!" she cried. "There IS a Santa Claus, isn't there?"

"Of course there's a Santa Claus," said Ma. She set the iron on the stove to heat again.

"The older you are, the more you know about Santa Claus," she said. "You are so big now, you know he can't be just one man, don't you? You know he is everywhere on Christmas Eve. He is in the Big Woods, and in Indian Territory, and far away in New York State, and here. He comes down all the chimneys at the same time. You know that, don't you?"

"Yes, Ma," said Mary and Laura.

"Well," said Ma. "Then you see—"

"I guess he is like angels," Mary said, slowly. And Laura could see that, just as well as Mary could.

Then Ma told them something else about Santa Claus. He was everywhere, and besides that, he was all the time.

Whenever anyone was unselfish, that was Santa Claus.

Christmas Eve was the time when everybody was unselfish. On that one night, Santa Claus was everywhere, because everybody, all together, stopped being selfish and wanted other people to be happy. And in the morning you saw what that had done.

"If everybody wanted everybody else to be happy, all the time, then would it be Christmas all the time?" Laura asked, and Ma said, "Yes, Laura."

Laura thought about that. So did Mary. They thought, and they looked at each other, and they knew what Ma wanted them to do. She wanted them to wish for nothing but horses for Pa. They looked at each other again and they looked away quickly and they did not say anything. Even Mary, who was always so good, did not say a word.

That night after supper Pa drew Laura and Mary close to him in the crook of his arms. Laura looked up at his face, and then she snuggled against him and said, "Pa."

"What is it, little half-pint of sweet cider?" Pa asked, and Laura said:

"Pa, I want Santa Claus—to bring—"

"What?" Pa asked.

"Horses," said Laura. "If you will let me ride them sometimes."

"So do I!" said Mary. But Laura had said it first.

Pa was surprised. His eyes shone soft and bright at them. "Would you girls really like horses?" he asked them.

"Oh yes, Pa!" they said.

"In that case," said Pa, smiling, "I have an idea that Santa Claus will bring us all a fine team of horses."

That settled it. They would not have any Christmas, only horses. Laura and Mary soberly undressed and soberly buttoned up their nightgowns and tied their nightcap strings. They knelt down together and said,

"Now I lay me down to sleep,

I pray the Lord my soul to keep.

If I should die before I wake

I pray the Lord my soul to take,

and please bless Pa and Ma and Carrie and everybody and make me a good girl for ever'n'ever. Amen."

Quickly Laura added, in her own head, "And please make me only glad about the Christmas horses, for ever'n'ever amen again."

She climbed into bed and almost right away she was glad. She thought of horses sleek and shining, of how their manes and tails blew in the wind, how they picked up their swift feet and sniffed the air with velvety noses and looked at everything with bright, soft eyes. And Pa would let her ride them.

Pa had tuned his fiddle and now he set it against his shoulder. Overhead the wind went wailing lonely in the cold dark. But in the dugout everything was snug and cosy.

Bits of fire-light came through the seams of the stove and twinkled on Ma's steel knitting needles and tried to catch Pa's elbow. In the shadows the bow was dancing, on the floor Pa's toe was tapping, and the merry music hid the lonely crying of the wind.

A Merry Christmas

Next morning, snow was in the air. Hard bits of snow were leaping and whirling in the howling wind.

Laura could not go out to play. In the stable, Spot and Pete and Bright stood all day long, eating the hay and straw. In the dugout, Pa mended his boots while Ma read to him again the story called *Millbank*. Mary sewed and Laura played with Charlotte. She could let Carrie hold Charlotte, but Carrie was too little to play with paper dolls; she might tear one.

That afternoon, when Carrie was asleep, Ma beckoned Mary and Laura. Her face was shining with a secret. They put their heads close to hers, and she told them. They could make a button-string for Carrie's Christmas!

They climbed onto their bed and turned their backs to Carrie and spread their laps wide. Ma brought them her button-box.

The box was almost full. Ma had saved buttons since she was smaller than Laura, and she had buttons her mother had saved when her mother was a little girl. There were blue buttons and red buttons, silvery and goldy buttons, curved-in buttons with tiny raised castles and bridges and trees on them, and twinkling jet buttons, painted china buttons, striped buttons, buttons like juicy blackberries, and even one tiny dog-head button. Laura squealed when she saw it.

"Sh!" Ma shushed her. But Carrie did not wake up.

Ma gave them all those buttons to make a button-string for Carrie.

After that, Laura did not mind staying in the dugout. When she saw the outdoors, the wind was driving snowdrifts across the bare frozen land. The creek was ice and the willow-tops rattled. In the dugout she and Mary had their secret.

They played gently with Carrie and gave her everything she wanted. They cuddled her and sang to her and got her to sleep whenever they could. Then they worked on the button-string.

Mary had one end of the string and Laura had the other. They picked out the buttons they wanted and strung them on the string. They held the string out and looked at it, and took off some buttons and put on others. Sometimes they took every button off, and started again. They were going to make the most beautiful button-string in the world.

One day Ma told them that this was the day before Christmas. They must finish the button-string that day.

They could not get Carrie to sleep. She ran and shouted, climbed on benches and jumped off, and skipped and sang. She did not get tired. Mary told her to sit still like a little lady, but she wouldn't. Laura let her hold Charlotte, and she jounced Charlotte up and down and flung her against the wall.

Finally Ma cuddled her and sang. Laura and Mary were perfectly still. Lower and lower Ma sang, and Carrie's eyes blinked till they shut. When softly Ma stopped singing, Carrie's eyes popped open and she shouted, "More, Ma! More!"

But at last she fell asleep. Then quickly, quickly, Laura and Mary finished the button-string. Ma tied the ends together for them. It was done;

they could not change one button more. It was a beautiful button-string.

That evening after supper, when Carrie was sound asleep, Ma hung her clean little pair of stockings from the table edge. Laura and Mary, in their nightgowns, slid the button-string into one stocking.

Then that was all. Mary and Laura were going to bed when Pa asked them, "Aren't you girls going to hang your stockings?"

"But I thought," Laura said, "I thought Santa Claus was going to bring us horses."

"Maybe he will," said Pa. "But little girls always hang up their stockings on Christmas Eve, don't they?"

Laura did not know what to think. Neither did Mary. Ma took two clean stockings out of the clothes-box, and Pa helped hang them beside Carrie's. Laura and Mary said their prayers and went to sleep, wondering.

In the morning Laura heard the fire crackling. She opened one eye the least bit, and saw lamplight, and a bulge in her Christmas stocking.

She yelled and jumped out of bed. Mary came running, too, and Carrie woke up. In Laura's stocking, and in Mary's stocking, there were little paper packages, just alike. In the packages was candy.

Laura had six pieces, and Mary had six. They had never seen such beautiful candy. It was too beautiful to eat. Some pieces were like ribbons, bent in waves. Some were short bits of round stick candy, and on their flat ends were colored flowers that went all the way through. Some were perfectly round and striped.

In one of Carrie's stockings were four pieces of that beautiful candy. In the other was the button-string. Carrie's eyes and her mouth were perfectly round when she saw it. Then she squealed, and grabbed it and squealed again. She sat on Pa's knee, looking at her candy and her button-string and wriggling and laughing with joy.

Then it was time for Pa to do the chores. He said, "Do you suppose there is anything for us in the stable?" And Ma said, "Dress as fast as you can, girls, and you can go to the stable and see what Pa finds."

It was winter, so they had to put on stockings and shoes. But Ma helped them button up the shoes and she pinned their shawls under their chins. They ran out into the cold.

Everything was gray, except a long red streak in the eastern sky. Its red light shone on the patches of gray-white snow. Snow was caught in the dead grass on the walls and roof of the stable and it was red. Pa stood waiting in the stable door. He laughed when he saw Laura and Mary, and he stepped outside to let them go in.

There, standing in Pete's and Bright's places, were two horses.

They were larger than Pet and Patty, and they were a soft, red-brown color, shining like silk. Their manes and tails were black. Their eyes were bright and gentle. They put their velvety noses down to Laura and nibbled softly at her hand and breathed warm on it.

"Well, flutterbudget!" said Pa. "And Mary. How do you girls like your Christmas?"

"Very much, Pa," said Mary, but Laura could only say, "Oh, Pa!"

Pa's eyes shone deep and he asked, "Who wants to ride the Christmas horses to water?"

Laura could hardly wait while he lifted Mary up and showed her how to hold on to the mane, and told her not to be afraid. Then Pa's strong hands swung Laura up. She sat on the horse's big, gentle back and felt its aliveness carrying her.

All outdoors was glittering now with sunshine on snow and frost. Pa went ahead, leading the horses and carrying his ax to break the ice in the creek so they could drink. The horses lifted their heads and took deep breaths and whooshed the cold out of their noses. Their velvety ears

pricked forward, then back and forward again.

Laura held to her horse's mane and clapped her shoes together and laughed. Pa and the horses and Mary and Laura were all happy in the gay, cold Christmas morning.

It's almost Christmastime at Plum Creek again, and Laura and Mary are working hard on their lessons in the new little house that Pa has built. Then one day there are no lessons, because Ma says that everyone must get dressed in order to go to town that night. Laura and Mary are astonished—they never ever go to town at night. But Ma will tell them only that they must not ask any more questions, for it is a Christmas surprise!

Surprise

That was another mild winter without much snow. It was still grasshopper weather. But chill winds blew, the sky was gray, and the best place for little girls was in the cosy house.

Pa was gone outdoors all day. He hauled logs and chopped them into wood for the stove. He followed frozen Plum Creek far upstream where nobody lived, and set traps along the banks for muskrat and otter and mink.

Every morning Laura and Mary studied their books and worked sums on the slate. Every afternoon Ma heard their lessons. She said they were good little scholars, and she was sure that when they went to school again they would find they had kept up with their classes.

Every Sunday they went to Sunday school. Laura saw Nellie Oleson showing off her fur cape. She remembered what Nellie had said about Pa, and she burned hot inside. She knew that hot feeling was wicked. She knew she must forgive Nellie, or she would never be an angel. She thought hard about the pictures of beautiful angels in the big paper-covered Bible at home. But they wore long white nightgowns. Not one of them wore a fur cape.

One happy Sunday was the Sunday when the Reverend Alden came from eastern Minnesota to preach in this western church. He preached for a long time, while Laura looked at his soft blue eyes and watched his beard wagging. She hoped he would speak to her after church. And he did.

"Here are my little country girls, Mary and Laura!" he said. He remembered their names.

Laura was wearing her new dress that day. The skirt was long enough, and the sleeves were long, too. They made her coat sleeves look shorter than ever, but the red braid on the cuffs was pretty.

"What a pretty new dress, Laura!" the Reverend Alden said.

Laura almost forgave Nellie Oleson that day. Then came Sundays when the Reverend Alden stayed at his own far church and in Sunday school Nellie Oleson turned up her nose at Laura and flounced her shoulders under the fur cape. Hot wickedness boiled up in Laura again.

One afternoon Ma said there would be no lessons, because they must all get ready to go to town that night. Laura and Mary were astonished.

"But we never go to town at night!" Mary said.

"There must always be a first time," said Ma.

"But why must there be, Ma?" Laura asked. "Why are we going to town at night?"

"It's a surprise," said Ma. "Now, no more questions. We must all take baths, and be our very nicest."

In the middle of the week, Ma brought in the washtub and heated water for Mary's bath. Then again for Laura's bath, and again for Carrie's. There had never been such scrubbing and scampering, such a changing to fresh drawers and petticoats, such brushing of shoes and braiding of hair and tying on of hair ribbons. There had never been such a wondering.

Supper was early. After supper, Pa bathed in the bedroom. Laura and Mary put on their new dresses. They knew better than to ask any more questions, but they wondered and whispered together.

The wagon box was full of clean hay. Pa put Mary and Laura in it and wrapped blankets around them. He climbed to the seat beside Ma and drove away toward town.

The stars were small and frosty in the dark sky. The horses' feet clippety-clopped and the wagon rattled over the hard ground.

Pa heard something else. "Whoa!" he said, pulling up the reins. Sam and David stopped. There was nothing but vast, dark coldness and stillness pricked by the stars. Then the stillness blossomed into the loveliest sound.

Two clear notes sounded, and sounded again and again.

No one moved. Only Sam and David tinkled their bits together and breathed. Those two notes went on, full and loud, soft and low. They seemed to be the stars singing.

Too soon Ma murmured, "We'd better be getting on, Charles," and the wagon rattled on. Still through its rattling Laura could hear those swaying notes.

"Oh, Pa, what is it?" she asked, and Pa said, "It's the new churchbell, Laura."

It was for this that Pa had worn his old patched boots.

The town seemed asleep. The stores were dark as Pa drove past them. Then Laura exclaimed, "Oh, look at the church! How pretty the church is!"

The church was full of light. Light spilled out of all its windows and ran out into the darkness from the door when it opened to let some one in. Laura almost jumped out from under the blankets before she remembered that she must never stand up in the wagon when the horses were going.

Pa drove to the church steps and helped them all out. He told them to go in, but they waited in the cold until he had covered Sam and David with their blankets. Then he came, and they all went into the church together.

Laura's mouth fell open and her eyes stretched to look at what she saw. She held Mary's hand tightly and they followed Ma and Pa. They sat down. Then Laura could look with all her might.

Standing in front of the crowded benches was a tree. Laura decided it must be a tree. She could see its trunk and branches. But she had never before seen such a tree.

Where leaves would be in summer, there were clusters and streamers

of thin green paper. Thick among them hung little sacks made of pink mosquito-bar. Laura was almost sure she could see candy in them. From the branches hung packages wrapped in colored paper, red packages and pink packages and yellow packages, all tied with colored string. Silk scarves were draped among them. Red mittens hung by the cord that would go around your neck and keep them from being lost if you were wearing them. A pair of new shoes hung by their heels from a branch. Lavish strings of white popcorn were looped all over this.

Under the tree and leaning against it were all kinds of things. Laura saw a crinkly-bright washboard, a wooden tub, a churn and dasher, a sled made of new boards, a shovel, a long-handled pitchfork.

Laura was too excited to speak. She squeezed Mary's hand tighter and tighter, and she looked up at Ma, wanting so much to know what that was. Ma smiled down at her and answered, "That is a Christmas tree, girls. Do you think it is pretty?"

They could not answer. They nodded while they kept on looking at that wonderful tree. They were hardly even surprised to know that this was Christmas, though they had not expected Christmas yet because there was not enough snow. Just then Laura saw the most wonderful thing of all. From a far branch of that tree hung a little fur cape, and a muff to match!

The Reverend Alden was there. He preached about Christmas, but Laura was looking at that tree and she could not hear what he said. Everyone stood up to sing and Laura stood up, but she could not sing. Not a sound would come out of her throat. In the whole world, there couldn't be a store so wonderful to look at as that tree.

After the singing, Mr. Tower and Mr. Beadle began taking things off it, and reading out names. Mrs. Tower and Miss Beadle brought those things down past the benches, and gave them to the person whose name was on them.

Everything on that tree was a Christmas present for somebody!

When Laura knew that, the lamps and people and voices and even the tree began to whirl. They whirled faster, noisier, and more excited. Some one gave her a pink mosquito-bar bag. It did have candy in it, and a big popcorn ball. Mary had one, too. So did Carrie. Every girl and boy had one. Then Mary had a pair of blue mittens. Then Laura had a red pair.

Ma opened a big package, and there was a warm, big, brown-and-red plaid shawl for her. Pa got a woolly muffler. Then Carrie had a rag doll with a china head. She screamed for joy. Through the laughing and talking and rustling of papers Mr. Beadle and Mr. Tower went on shouting names.

The little fur cape and muff still hung on the tree, and Laura wanted them. She wanted to look at them as long as she could. She wanted to know who got them. They could not be for Nellie Oleson who already had a fur cape.

Laura did not expect anything more. But to Mary came a pretty little booklet with Bible pictures in it, from Mrs. Tower.

Mr. Tower was taking the little fur cape and the muff from the tree. He read a name, but Laura could not hear it through all the joyful noise. She lost sight of the cape and muff among all the people. They were gone now.

Then to Carrie came a cunning little brown-spotted white china dog. But Carrie's arms and her eyes were full of her doll. So Laura held and stroked and laughed over the sleek little dog.

"Merry Christmas, Laura!" Miss Beadle said, and in Laura's hand she put a beautiful little box. It was made of snow-white, gleaming china. On its top stood a wee, gold-colored teapot and a gold-colored tiny cup in a gold-colored saucer.

The top of the box lifted off. Inside was a nice place to keep a breast-pin, if some day Laura had a breast-pin. Ma said it was a jewel-box.

There had never been such a Christmas as this. It was such a large, rich Christmas, the whole church full of Christmas. There were so many lamps, so many people, so much noise and laughter, and so many happinesses in it. Laura felt full and bursting, as if that whole big rich Christmas were inside her, and her mittens and her beautiful jewel-box with the wee gold cup-and-saucer and teapot, and her candy and her popcorn ball. And suddenly some one said, "These are for you, Laura."

Mrs. Tower stood smiling, holding out the little fur cape and muff.

"For me?" Laura said. "For me?" Then everything else vanished while with both arms she hugged the soft furs to her.

She hugged them tighter and tighter, trying to believe they were really hers, that silky-soft little brown fur cape and the muff.

All around her Christmas went on, but Laura knew only the softness of those furs. People were going home. Carrie was standing on the bench while Ma fastened her coat and tied her hood more snugly. Ma was saying,

"Thank you so much for the shawl, Brother Alden. It is just what I needed."

Pa said, "And I thank you for the muffler. It will feel good when I come to town in the cold."

The Reverend Alden sat down on the bench and asked, "And does Mary's coat fit?"

Laura had not noticed Mary's coat until then. Mary had on a new dark-blue coat. It was long, and its sleeves came down to Mary's wrists. Mary buttoned it up, and it fitted.

"And how does this little girl like her furs?" the Reverend Alden smiled. He drew Laura between his knees. He laid the fur cape around her shoulders and fastened it at the throat. He put the cord of the muff around her neck, and her hands went inside the silky muff.

"There!" the Reverend Alden said. "Now my little country girls will be warm when they come to Sunday school."

"What do you say, Laura?" Ma asked, but the Reverend Alden said, "There is no need. The way her eyes are shining is enough."

Laura could not speak. The golden-brown fur cuddled her neck and softly hugged her shoulders. Down her front it hid the threadbare fastenings of her coat. The muff came far up her wrists and hid the shortness of her coat sleeves.

"She's a little brown bird with red trimmings," the Reverend Alden said.

Then Laura laughed. It was true. Her hair and her coat, her dress and the wonderful furs, were brown. Her hood and mittens and the braid on her dress were red.

"I'll tell my church people back east about our little brown bird," said the Reverend Alden. "You see, when I told them about our church out here, they said they must send a box for the Christmas tree. They all gave things they had. The little girls who sent your furs and Mary's coat needed larger ones."

"Thank you, sir," said Laura. "And please, sir, tell them thank you, too." For when she could speak, her manners were as nice as Mary's.

Then they all said good night and Merry Christmas to the Reverend Alden. Mary was so beautiful in her Christmas coat. Carrie was so pretty on Pa's arm. Pa and Ma were smiling so happily and Laura was all gladness.

Mr. and Mrs. Oleson were going home, too. Mr. Oleson's arms were full of things, and so were Nellie's and Willie's. No wickedness boiled up in Laura now; she only felt a little bit of mean gladness.

"Merry Christmas, Nellie," Laura said. Nellie stared, while Laura walked quietly on, with her hands snuggled deep in the soft muff. Her cape was prettier than Nellie's, and Nellie had no muff.

Christmas is coming once again to Plum Creek, but Laura doesn't feel much like celebrating. A terrible blizzard has been roaring around the little house on the banks of Plum Creek for four days now. Worst of all, Pa left for town a few hours before the storm began, and he still has not come home. Laura, Mary, and Ma are sure that he must have stayed in town, but they are anxiously waiting for him all the same. And it's Christmas Eve—will Pa make it home safely and in time for Christmas?

The Fourth Day

In the morning those sounds were gone from the wind. It was blowing with a steady wailing scream and the house stood still. But the roaring fire in the stove gave hardly any heat.

"The cold is worse," Ma said. "Don't try to do the housework properly. Wrap up in your shawls and keep Carrie with you close to the stove."

Soon after Ma came back from the stable, the frost on the eastern window glowed faintly yellow. Laura ran to breathe on it and scratch away the ice until she made a peep-hole. Outdoors the sun was shining!

Ma looked out, then Mary and Laura took turns looking out at the snow blowing in waves over the ground. The sky looked like ice. Even the air looked cold above that fast-blowing flood of snow, and the sunshine that came through the peep-hole was no warmer than a shadow.

Sidewise from the peep-hole, Laura glimpsed something dark. A furry big animal was wading deep in the blowing snow. A bear, she thought. It shambled behind the corner of the house and darkened the front window.

"Ma!" she cried. The door opened, the snowy, furry animal came in. Pa's eyes looked out of its face. Pa's voice said, "Have you been good girls while I was gone?"

Ma ran to him. Laura and Mary and Carrie ran, crying and laughing. Ma helped him out of his coat. The fur was full of snow that showered on the floor. Pa let the coat drop, too.

"Charles! You're frozen!" Ma said.

"Just about," said Pa. "And I'm hungry as a wolf. Let me sit down by the fire, Caroline, and feed me."

His face was thin and his eyes large. He sat shivering, close to the oven, and said he was only cold, not frost-bitten. Ma quickly warmed some of the bean broth and gave it to him.

"That's good," he said. "That warms a fellow."

Ma pulled off his boots and he put his feet up to the heat from the oven.

"Charles," Ma asked, "did you— Were you—" She stood smiling with her mouth trembling.

"Now, Caroline, don't you ever worry about me," said Pa. "I'm bound to come home to take care of you and the girls." He lifted Carrie to his knee, and put an arm around Laura, and the other around Mary. "What did you think, Mary?"

"I thought you would come," Mary answered.

"That's the girl! And you, Laura?"

"I didn't think you were with Mr. Fitch telling stories," said Laura. "I—I kept wishing hard."

"There you are, Caroline! How could a fellow fail to get home?" Pa asked Ma. "Give me some more of that broth, and I'll tell you all about it."

They waited while he rested, and ate bean broth with bread, and drank hot tea. His hair and his beard were wet with snow melting in them. Ma dried them with a towel. He took her hand and drew her down beside him and asked:

"Caroline, do you know what this weather means? It means we'll have a bumper crop of wheat next year!"

"Does it, Charles?" said Ma.

"We won't have any grasshoppers next summer. They say in town that grasshoppers come only when the summers are hot and dry and the winters are mild. We are getting so much snow now that we're bound to have fine crops next year."

"That's good, Charles," Ma said, quietly.

"Well, they were talking about all this in the store, but I knew I ought to start home. Just as I was leaving, Fitch showed me the buffalo coat. He got it cheap from a man who went east on the last train running, and had to have money to buy his ticket. Fitch said I could have the coat for ten dollars. Ten dollars is a lot of money, but—"

"I'm glad you got the coat, Charles," said Ma.

"As it turned out, it's lucky I did, though I didn't know it then. But going to town, the wind went right through me. It was cold enough to freeze the nose off a brass monkey. And seemed like my old coat didn't even strain that wind. So when Fitch told me to pay him when I sell my trapped furs next spring, I put that buffalo coat on over my old one.

"As soon as I was out on the prairie I saw the cloud in the north-west, but it was so small and far away that I thought I could beat it home. Pretty soon I began to run, but I was no more than halfway when the storm struck me. I couldn't see my hand before my face.

"It would be all right if these blizzard winds didn't come from all directions at once. I don't know how they do it. When a storm comes from the north-west, a man ought to be able to go straight north by keeping the wind on his left cheek. But a fellow can't do anything like that in a blizzard.

"Still, it seemed I ought to be able to walk straight ahead, even if I couldn't see or tell directions. So I kept on walking, straight ahead, I thought. Till I knew I was lost. I had come a good two miles without getting to the creek, and I had no idea which way to turn. The only thing to do was to keep on going. I had to walk till the storm quit. If I stopped I'd freeze.

"So I set myself to outwalk the storm. I walked and walked. I could not see any more than if I had been stone blind. I could hear nothing but the wind. I kept on walking in that white blur. I don't know if you noticed, there seem to be voices howling and things screaming overhead, in a blizzard?"

"Yes, Pa, I heard them!" Laura said.

"So did I," said Mary. And Ma nodded.

"And balls of fire," said Laura.

"Balls of fire?" Pa asked.

"That will keep, Laura," said Ma. "Go on, Charles. What did you do?"

"I kept on walking," Pa answered. "I walked till the white blur turned gray and then black, and I knew it was night. I figured I had been walking four hours, and these blizzards last three days and nights. But I kept on walking."

Pa stopped, and Ma said, "I had the lamp burning in the window for you."

"I didn't see it," said Pa. "I kept straining my eyes to see something, but all I saw was the dark. Then of a sudden, everything gave way under me and I went straight down, must have been ten feet. It seemed farther.

"I had no idea what had happened or where I was. But I was out of the wind. The blizzard was yelling and shrieking overhead, but the air was fairly still where I was. I felt around me. There was snow banked up as high as I could reach on three sides of me, and the other side was a kind of wall of bare ground, sloping back at the bottom.

"It didn't take me long to figure that I'd walked off the bank of some gully, somewhere on the prairie. I crawled back under the bank, and there I was with solid ground at my back and overhead, snug as a bear in a den. I didn't believe I would freeze there, out of the wind and with the buffalo coat to keep warmth in my body. So I curled up in it and went to sleep, being pretty tired.

"My, I was glad I had that coat, and a good warm cap with earlaps, and that extra pair of thick socks, Caroline.

"When I woke up I could hear the blizzard, but faintly. There was solid snow in front of me, coated over with ice where my breath had melted it. The blizzard had filled up the hole I had made when I fell. There must have been six feet of snow over me, but the air was good. I moved my arms and legs and fingers and toes, and felt my nose and ears to make sure I was not freezing. I could still hear the storm, so I went to sleep again.

"How long has it been, Caroline?"

"Three days and nights," said Ma. "This is the fourth day."

Then Pa asked Mary and Laura, "Do you know what day this is?"

"Is it Sunday?" Mary guessed.

"It's the day before Christmas," said Ma.

Laura and Mary had forgotten all about Christmas. Laura asked, "Did you sleep all that time, Pa?"

"No," said Pa. "I kept on sleeping and waking up hungry, and sleeping some more, till I woke up just about starved. I was bringing home some oyster crackers for Christmas. They were in a pocket of the buffalo coat. I took a handful of those crackers out of the paper bag and ate them. I felt out in the snow and took a handful, and I ate that for a drink. Then all I could do was lie there and wait for the storm to stop.

"I tell you, Caroline, it was mighty hard to do that, thinking of you and the girls and knowing you would go out in the blizzard to do the chores. But I knew I could not get home till the blizzard stopped.

"So I waited a long time, till I was so hungry again that I ate all the rest of the oyster crackers. They were no bigger than the end of my thumb. One of them wasn't half a mouthful, and the whole half-pound of them wasn't very filling.

"Then I went on waiting, sleeping some. I guessed it was night again. Whenever I woke I listened closely, and I could hear the dim sound of the

blizzard. I could tell by that sound that the snow was getting thicker over me, but the air was still good in my den. The heat of my blood was keeping me from freezing.

"I tried to sleep all I could, but I was so hungry that I kept waking up. Finally I was too hungry to sleep at all. Girls, I was bound and determined I would not do it, but after some time I did. I took the paper bag out of the inside pocket of my old overcoat, and I ate every bit of the Christmas candy. I'm sorry."

Laura hugged him from one side and Mary hugged him from the other. They hugged him hard and Laura said, "Oh Pa, I am so glad you did!"

"So am I, Pa! So am I!" said Mary. They were truly glad.

"Well," Pa said, "we'll have a big wheat crop next year, and you girls won't have to wait till next Christmas for candy."

"Was it good, Pa?" Laura asked. "Did you feel better after you ate it?"

"It was very good, and I felt much better," said Pa. "I went right to sleep and I must have slept most of yesterday and last night. Suddenly I sat up wide awake. I could not hear a sound.

"Now, was I buried so deep in snow that I couldn't hear the blizzard, or had it stopped? I listened hard. It was so still that I could hear the silence.

"Girls, I began digging on that snow like a badger. I wasn't slow in digging up out of that den. I came scrabbling through the top of that snow bank, and where do you suppose I was?

"I was on the bank of Plum Creek, just above the place where we set the fish-trap, Laura."

"Why, I can see that place from the window," said Laura.

"Yes. And I could see this house," said Pa. All that long, terrible time he had been so near. The lamp in the window had not been able to shine into the blizzard at all, or he would have seen its light.

"My legs were so stiff and cramped that I could hardly stand on them," said Pa. "But I saw this house and I started for home just as fast as I could go. And here I am!" he finished, hugging Laura and Mary.

Then he went to the big buffalo coat and he took out of one of its pockets a flat, square-edge can of bright tin. He asked, "What do you think I have brought you for Christmas dinner?"

They could not guess.

"Oysters!" said Pa. "Nice, fresh oysters! They were frozen solid when

I got them, and they are frozen solid yet. Better put them in the lean-to, Caroline, so they will stay that way till tomorrow."

Laura touched the can. It was cold as ice.

"I ate up the oyster crackers, and I ate up the Christmas candy, but by jinks," said Pa, "I brought the oysters home!"

Christmas Eve

Pa went early to do the chores that evening, and Jack went with him, staying close to his heels. Jack did not intend to lose sight of Pa again.

They came in, cold and snowy. Pa stamped the snow from his feet and hung his old coat with his cap on the nail by the lean-to door. "The wind is rising again," he said. "We will have another blizzard before morning."

"Just so you are here, Charles, I don't care how much it storms," said Ma.

Jack lay down contentedly and Pa sat warming his hands by the stove.

"Laura," he said, "if you'll bring me the fiddle-box I'll play you a tune."

Laura brought the fiddle-box to him. Pa tuned the fiddle and rosined the bow, and then while Ma cooked supper he filled the house with music.

> *"Oh, Charley he's a fine young man,*
>
> *Oh, Charley he's a dandy!*
>
> *Charley likes to kiss the girls*
>
> *And he can do it handy!*
>
> *"I don't want none of your weevily wheat,*
>
> *I don't want none of your barley,*
>
> *I want fine flour in half an hour,*
>
> *To bake a cake for Charley!"*

Pa's voice rollicked with the rollicking tune, and Carrie laughed and clapped her hands, and Laura's feet were dancing.

Then the fiddle changed the tune and Pa began to sing about sweet Lily Dale.

> *"'Twas a calm, still night,*
>
> *And the moon's pale light*
>
> *Shone soft o'er hill and dale. . . ."*

Pa glanced at Ma, busy at the stove, while Mary and Laura sat listening, and the fiddle slipped into frolicking up and down with his voice.

> *"Mary put the dishes on,*
> *The dishes on, the dishes on,*
> *Mary put the dishes on,*
> *We'll all take tea!"*

"And what shall I do, Pa?" Laura cried, while Mary ran to get the plates and cups from the cupboard. The fiddle and Pa kept singing, down all the steps they had just gone up.

> *"Laura take them off again,*
> *Off again, off again,*
> *Laura clear the table when*
> *We've all gone away!"*

So Laura knew that Mary was to set the table for supper and she was to clear away afterward.

The wind was screaming fiercer and louder outside. Snow whirled swish-swishing against the windows. But Pa's fiddle sang in the warm, lamp-lighted house. The dishes made small clinking sounds as Mary set the table. Carrie rocked herself in the rocking-chair and Ma went gently between the table and the stove. In the middle of the table she set a milk-pan full of beautiful brown baked beans, and now from the oven she took the square baking-pan full of golden corn-bread. The rich brown smell and the sweet golden smell curled deliciously together in the air.

Pa's fiddle laughed and sang,

> *"I'm Captain Jinks of the Horse Marines,*
> *I feed my horse on corn and beans*
> *Although 'tis far beyond my means, for*
> *I'm Captain Jinks of the Horse Marines!*
> *I'm Captain of the army!"*

Laura patted Jack's furry smooth forehead and scratched his ears for him, and then with both hands she gave his head a quick, happy squeeze. Everything was so good. Grasshoppers were gone, and next year Pa could harvest the wheat. Tomorrow was Christmas, with oyster stew for dinner.

There would be no presents and no candy, but Laura could not think of anything she wanted and she was so glad that the Christmas candy had helped to bring Pa safe home again.

"Supper is ready," Ma said in her gentle voice.

Pa laid the fiddle in its box. He stood up and looked around at them all. His blue eyes shone at them.

"Look, Caroline," he said, "how Laura's eyes are shining."

Merry, Merry Christmas!

(A Christmas Carol)
Words and Music by Mrs. T. J. Cook

Mer-ry, mer-ry Christ-mas ev-'ry-where! Cheer-i-ly it ring-eth

through the air; Christ-mas bells, Christ-mas trees,

Christ-mas o-dors on the breeze, Mer-ry, mer-ry Christ-mas

ev-'ry-where! Cheer-i-ly it ring-eth through the air.

Verse

1. Why should we so joy-ful-ly   Sing with grate-ful   mirth?
2. Light for wea-ry wan-der-ers,   Com-fort for th' op-pressed!
3. Deeds of Faith and Char-i - ty,   These our off-'rings   be,

See, the Sun of Right-eous-ness Beams up-on the   earth!
He will guide His trust-ing ones In - to per-fect rest.
Lead-ing ev - 'ry soul to sing   Christ was born for me!